Castle of Schemes
and Dreams

ALSO BY JOE McGEE

NIGHT FRIGHTS
The Haunted Mustache
The Lurking Lima Bean
The Not-So-Itsy-Bitsy Spider
The Squirrels Have Gone Nuts

JUNIOR MONSTER SCOUTS
The Monster Squad
Crash! Bang! Boo!
It's Raining Bats and Frogs!
Monster of Disguise
Trash Heap of Terror
Curse of the Crummy Mummy!
Chiller Thriller!
The Rottenest Reunion
The Incredible Shrinking Grump

JUNIOR MONSTER SCOUTS

#10 Castle of Schemes and Dreams

By Joe McGee
Illustrated by Ethan Long

ALADDIN
NEW YORK   AMSTERDAM/ANTWERP   LONDON
TORONTO   SYDNEY/MELBOURNE   NEW DELHI

If you purchased this book without a cover, you should be aware that this book is stolen property. It was reported as "unsold and destroyed" to the publisher, and neither the author nor the publisher has received any payment for this "stripped book."

This book is a work of fiction. Any references to historical events, real people, or real places are used fictitiously. Other names, characters, places, and events are products of the author's imagination, and any resemblance to actual events or places or persons, living or dead, is entirely coincidental.

ALADDIN

An imprint of Simon & Schuster Children's Publishing Division
1230 Avenue of the Americas, New York, New York 10020
For more than 100 years, Simon & Schuster has championed authors and the stories they create. By respecting the copyright of an author's intellectual property, you enable Simon & Schuster and the author to continue publishing exceptional books for years to come. We thank you for supporting the author's copyright by purchasing an authorized edition of this book. No amount of this book may be reproduced or stored in any format, nor may it be uploaded to any website, database, language-learning model, or other repository, retrieval, or artificial intelligence system without express permission. All rights reserved. Inquiries may be directed to Simon & Schuster, 1230 Avenue of the Americas, New York, NY 10020
or permissions@simonandschuster.com.
First Aladdin paperback edition May 2025
Text © 2025 by Joseph McGee | Illustrations © 2025 by Ethan Long
Also available in an Aladdin hardcover edition.
All rights reserved, including the right of reproduction in whole or in part in any form.
ALADDIN and related logo are registered trademarks of Simon & Schuster, LLC.
For information about special discounts for bulk purchases, please contact
Simon & Schuster Special Sales at 1-866-506-1949 or business@simonandschuster.com.
Simon & Schuster strongly believes in freedom of expression and stands against censorship in all its forms. For more information, visit BooksBelong.com.
The Simon & Schuster Speakers Bureau can bring authors to your live event.
For more information or to book an event, contact the Simon & Schuster Speakers Bureau at 1-866-248-3049 or visit our website at www.simonspeakers.com.
Cover design by Alicia Mikles based on series design by Karin Paprocki
Interior design by Mike Rosamilia
The illustrations for this book were rendered digitally.
The text of this book was set in Centaur MT.
Manufactured in the United States of America 0325 BID
2 4 6 8 10 9 7 5 3 1
Library of Congress Cataloging-in-Publication Data
Names: McGee, Joe, 1972– author. | Long, Ethan, illustrator.
Title: Castle of schemes and dreams / by Joe McGee ; illustrated by Ethan Long.
Description: New York : Aladdin, 2025. | Series: Junior Monster Scouts ; 10 | Audience: Ages 7 to 10 | Summary: Beloved Castle Dracula is in danger of being turned into a gigantic amusement park, so the Junior Monster Scouts, the villagers, and Baron Von Grump band together to save their little world from being turned upside down.
Identifiers: LCCN 2024043338 (print) | LCCN 2024043339 (ebook) |
ISBN 9781665956406 (hc) | ISBN 9781665956390 (pbk) | ISBN 9781665956413 (ebook)
Subjects: CYAC: Monsters—Fiction. | Castles—Fiction. | Humorous stories. | LCGFT: Humorous fiction. | Picture books.
Classification: LCC PZ7.1.M435 Cas 2025 (print) | LCC PZ7.1.M435 (ebook) | DDC [E]—dc23
LC record available at https://lccn.loc.gov/2024043338
LC ebook record available at https://lccn.loc.gov/2024043339

For Jessica: my best friend, my love, my wife,
my shield maiden, and my castle of dreams
—J. M.

★ ★ ★ ★

· THE SCOUTS ·

VAMPYRA may be a vampire, but that doesn't mean she wants your blood. Gross! In fact, she doesn't even like ketchup! She loves gymnastics, especially cartwheels, and one of her favorite things is hanging upside down... even when she's *not* a bat. She loves garlic in her food and sleeps in past noon, preferring the nighttime over the day. She lives in Castle Dracula with her mom, dad (Dracula), and aunts, who are always after her to brush her fangs and clean her cape.

WOLFY and his family live high in the mountains above Castle Dracula, where they can get the best view of the moon. He likes to hike and play in the creek and gaze at the stars. He especially likes to fetch sticks with his dad, Wolf Man, and go on family pack runs, even if he has to put up with all of his little brothers and sisters. They're always howling when he tries to talk! Mom says he has his father's fur. Boy, is he proud of that!

FRANKY STEIN has always been bigger than the other monsters. But it's not just his body that's big. It's his brain and his heart as well. He has plenty of hugs and smiles to go around. His dad, Frankenstein, is the scoutmaster, and one of Franky's favorite things is his well-worn Junior Monster Scout handbook. One day Franky is going to be a scoutmaster, like his dad. But for now . . . he wants a puppy. Dad says he'll make Franky one soon. Mom says Franky has to keep his workshop clean for a week first.

CASTLE

GRAVEYARD

CROOKED TRAIL

STARGAZER'S POINT

VILLAGE

WATERFALL

CHAPTER 1

WELCOME, DEAR READER! SETTLE IN with this book and a tasty cinnamon stroogle noodle (a kind of cinnamon-sugar-flavored pastry that is long and hollow and filled with cream cheese). Grab a nice glass of jamberry juice and put on your comfiest slippers. Relax and listen to the peaceful sounds of—

WHUMP-WHUMP-WHUMP-WHUMP-WHUMP.

What in the five flippers of frog flowers is that noise?

WHUMP-WHUMP-WHUMP-WHUMP-WHUMP.

That's *exactly* what Vampyra, Franky, and Wolfy said (well, almost). They were outside, enjoying the day and playing a game of "race your shadow"—where you run from one point to another, trying to outrace your shadow, which never seems to work and generally leaves you tired and out of breath.

"What is that noise?" Wolfy asked, covering his ears. He had very good hearing, so the noise was even louder for him.

WHUMP-WHUMP-WHUMP-WHUMP-WHUMP.

"Look," said Vampyra, pointing up into the sky. "A helicopter!"

"That's strange," said Franky. "I wonder who it is."

Franky, Wolfy, and Vampyra watched the helicopter pass over them, then over the Gloomy Woods and the covered bridge.

"Only one way to find out," said Franky.

"Let's go see who's whump-whump-whumping around here and disturbing the peace," said Vampyra.

Wolfy nodded. "And hurting my ears!"

. . .

The Junior Monster Scouts weren't the only ones interrupted by the whump-whump-whumping of the helicopter.

Someone else was equally disturbed. Perhaps even *more* disturbed. So disturbed that he leaped up out of his favorite chair, marched straight to the window, and threw open the shutters.

"What is the meaning of this noise!?" shouted Baron Von Grump.

But his voice—

WHUMP-WHUMP-WHUMP-WHUMP-WHUMP.

His voice was drowned out by—

WHUMP-WHUMP-WHUMP-WHUMP-WHUMP.

You get the idea.

The helicopter circled the windmill and then flew away.

Baron Von Grump shook his fist at the departing helicopter.

"Good riddance!" he said.

Edgar, his friend and pet raven, settled on the sill. He ruffled his feathers.

"Caw!" he said. That meant "And don't come back!"

But the helicopter wasn't leaving. The helicopter was landing.

Right in the middle of the village!

CHAPTER 2

YOU CAN PROBABLY IMAGINE WHAT A big deal this was for the villagers. A helicopter had never ever even flown by, let alone landed. But here it was, settling down on the grass. The villagers emerged from their homes, gawking and pointing. Even the cows and goats came up to their fences to see what was going on. The mayor combed his mustache, not once, but thrice, before going out to greet whoever was important enough to be landing a helicopter in their village.

It was a shiny, fancy, bright blue helicopter with the words FUN PARK! written across the side. The blades slowly stopped whirring and then the side door opened. A set of steps unfolded, and a man in a suit and tie stepped down. He smiled at the mayor, and the villagers, and the cows and goats. When he smiled, the sun glinted off his extremely white teeth. Every single piece of hair was in perfect position. He adjusted his top button and said in a very smooth, very pleasant voice, "Hello there, people of—" He turned back to a shorter man with very thick glasses, who held a clipboard and a briefcase.

"The village," said the shorter man with the very thick glasses.

"The village," said the man with the perfect hair and teeth. "My name is Gilbert Rutherford Weatherspan the Third, and I represent the Fun Park company. You want to have fun? Well then, look no further. We provide more fun than you could ever imagine!"

There were some *oohs* and *aahs* from the crowd.

"I want to have fun," said a beet farmer, leaning forward on his pitchfork.

"Me too," said a woman balancing a basket of bunnies on one hip and a baby on the other. "I could always go for some good old-fashioned fun."

"Can't get enough of it!" said an old man, scratching his beard. "Don't know what kind of fun you're talking about, but I'm all ears!"

Gilbert clapped his hands and smiled again at the crowd. "Well, you're in luck," he said. "Because Fun Park is going to open a new amusement park right next to your village!"

"You are?" asked the mayor.

"We are!" said Gilbert. "Rides, games,

food, and fun. More fun than you can shake a stick at."

"Now you're talking!" said the beet farmer.

"And in order to bring in all this fabulous fun, we're going to build roads and bridges and bypasses—"

"And tunnels," added the shorter man with the very thick glasses, whose name is Arthur, so we don't have to keep calling him the shorter man with the very thick glasses.

"And tunnels," said Gilbert. "And even an airport, so we can fly people in from all over the world!"

"An airport?" asked the woman with the bunnies and the baby. "Here?"

"Oh yes," said Gilbert. "How else can people from all over the world come and enjoy the fun?"

"That sounds like . . . a lot," said the mayor. He was suddenly not so sure about this.

"You just wait and see, my good man," said Gilbert. "Fun Park will change the way you live!"

The mayor groaned and clutched his hat.

"That's what I'm worried about," he said.

But nobody was listening. The rest of the villagers were too busy dreaming about all the fun they were going to have and admiring Gilbert's fantastic hair and beautiful teeth.

Gilbert climbed back into the helicopter.

"Lots to do, plans to make. Oh, one more thing . . . that castle . . ." He pointed to Castle Dracula. "Who happens to own that wonderful castle?"

"Why, that belongs to Count Dracula," said the mayor.

"A count, eh?" said Gilbert. "Make a note, Arthur. A nobleman. We'll have to make him an exceptional offer."

"An offer for what?" asked the mayor.

"To buy it, of course," laughed Gilbert. "That is the *perfect* spot for Fun Park. A castle-themed amusement park! There will be roller coasters and rides galore, like the Dueling Dragons roller coaster, which has two roller coasters spinning around each other at the same time, or the Wizard's

Whipsy Whoozie, sure to make your hair stand on end. And let's not forget the Spinny Bajingy, or the Tower Twister, a marvel of heights and frights! There will be games and food and jugglers on stilts. There will be parades and performances and fireworks each and every night. All right there, in and around that castle. Good day, simple villagers!"

He closed the helicopter door, the stairs folded up, and the helicopter lifted off into the air.

CHAPTER 3

VAMPYRA, WOLFY, AND FRANKY HAD just reached the village as the helicopter flew away.

"Hello, Mister Mayor," Franky said. "What was that about?"

"Oh dear," said the mayor. "I'm afraid the castle is in danger!"

"Danger?" Wolfy asked.

"Danger!" said the mayor.

"In danger of becoming fun!" said the beet farmer.

"More fun than we can shake a stick at!" said the woman with the baby and the basket of bunnies.

"Rides, games, and fun galore!" said the old man with the beard.

The Junior Monster Scouts did not know what to make of this. It sounded a bit confusing. The mayor was talking about danger, yet somehow, the villagers were excited about it.

"What's the danger?" Vampyra asked. "And what does it have to do with the castle?"

"Fun Park wants to buy Castle Dracula!" said the mayor. "They're going to turn it into an amusement park!"

Vampyra, Wolfy, and Franky about fell over. Buy Castle Dracula? Turn it into an amusement park? That was preposterous! Think of all the plans that were formed in the castle to help the villagers. Think of the experiments and inventions created in the tower. Think of all the scout meetings, and friendships, and goodwill that came from Castle Dracula and the monsters who lived there. Castle Dracula was the heartbeat of the whole valley.

"We'd better get back to the castle," said Vampyra.

"Don't worry, Mister Mayor," said Franky, "we won't let Fun Park walk in here and take over."

"But I have a feeling it's going to take *all* of us to stop it from happening," said Wolfy.

"All of us?" the mayor asked.

Wolfy nodded. "Monsters, villagers . . .

and"—he looked in the direction of the windmill—"maybe even Baron Von Grump."

And speaking of Baron Von Grump . . . he had just settled back down into his favorite chair, with no more WHUMP-WHUMPing of the helicopter, when another noise sprang up. This was a BEEP-BEEP-BEEPing of several large work trucks and machines. There were steamrollers and dump trucks, bulldozers and cranes, concrete mixers and forklifts, and a bunch of men and women in hard hats with clipboards.

Baron Von Grump charged out of his windmill, and Edgar flew right along with him.

"WHAT is the meaning of this?" Baron

Von Grump hollered. He even shook his fist! He was quite perturbed. "I demand an explanation! Remove your trucks and your clipboards and your hard hats and . . . stop this blasted noise!"

"Caw!" Edgar added. That meant "At once!"

A woman in a hard hat lowered her clipboard and shook her head.

"I'm afraid we can't do that," she said. "We've got a road to build."

"A road?" asked Baron Von Grump.

"A road," she said. "A big road too. Lots of lanes in both directions."

"Here?" asked Baron Von Grump.

She looked at her clipboard and nodded.

"Right here," she said. "Passing next to your windmill, then looping back around the cheese factory and over and around the village, and up to that castle over yonder. Of course, there will be exits and off-ramps for the Fun Park parking lots and the Fun Park hotels . . . oh, and for the airport that'll be going right over there."

She pointed to Stargazer's Point, where the Trash Heap and her children lived.

Baron Von Grump tugged on his beard. He pulled at his mustache. Finally, he stamped his foot.

"I won't allow it!" he said.

"Caw!" said Edgar. That meant "Neither will I!"

The lady with the hard hat and clipboard unrolled a large blueprint.

"I'm sorry to say that you have no choice. All this land besides here, here, here, and here now belongs to the Fun Park Corporation."

She pointed to the windmill, the village, the Cheese Storage Pyramid, and Castle Dracula.

"And Fun Park wants roads, bridges, bypasses, and an airport," she said.

A man with an armful of blueprints leaned in and whispered in her ear.

"And tunnels," she added. "What Fun Park wants, Fun Park gets."

Baron Von Grump suddenly felt very, very dizzy.

CHAPTER 4

VAMPYRA, FRANKY, AND WOLFY RACED back to Castle Dracula as fast as they could.

Gilbert's helicopter was just leaving, and Dracula, Frankenstein, and Wolf Man were standing outside. They looked very upset.

"Dad!" said Vampyra. "What did he say?"

She watched the helicopter fly off into the distance.

"He wants to turn Castle Dracula into an amusement park," said Frankenstein.

"But it's not his castle," said Wolfy.

"He said that if we didn't sell it to him, he'd be forced to take it!" said Dracula.

"Take it?" Vampyra asked. "He can't just take Castle Dracula! This is our home. Some of our greatest ideas have come from here, in the halls and towers of our castle. This is where the Junior Monster Scouts help people when they're in need."

"He said that he'd have the board of health force us out because of the rats, and the cobwebs, and the potions, and the laboratory," said Wolf Man. "He said the experiments were dangerous, the rats were an infestation, and the potions were unstable."

Wolf Man let out a long, sad howl.

Wolfy's little sister Fern and the rest

of the Little Junior Monster Scouts heard Wolf Man's sad howl, and they joined the gathered monsters. When they heard what was going on, they got very upset.

Fern put her paws on her hips and said, in a very serious voice, "We have to orphanize a town meeting!"

"Don't you mean *organize?*" Wolfy asked.

Fern threw her paws up in the air. "That's what I said!"

Boris and the rats had also come to join the gathered monsters. Boris was the leader of the rats who lived in the basement of Castle Dracula.

"A meeting," he said, munching on a big hunk of cheese. "That's a good idea, kid. Whaddaya think, fellas?"

The other rats all nodded in agreement.

I'm nodding too. Are you nodding? Do you want to be part of the meeting to save Castle Dracula and the village? I thought so. Well, good thing you're right here, reading this book, because when the meeting happens, you'll be the first one there! And I know you can't even imagine Castle Dracula not being . . . well, Castle Dracula! Where else can we expect to have scout meetings and lab experiments and invented gadgets and soaring gargoyles?

"We'll need to get everyone together," said Franky. "The villagers, the Trash Heap, and even Baron Von Grump. It's only a matter of time before Gilbert's workers move in and try to take Castle Dracula from us. It's not just a building, or our home; it's part of who we *are*. It's part of what makes us Monster Scouts. It inspires and energizes us!"

"It might already be too late," Dracula moaned. He pointed down the Crooked Trail to where bulldozers rumbled toward the Gloomy Woods.

"Wow," said Wolf Man. "This guy moves fast."

Wolf Man has a point. That was pretty quick. Gilbert must have been planning this for a while. Why that scoundrel, Gilbert Rutherford Weatherspan the Third! I'd have a thing or two to say to him if he were here right now. He makes me so mad! Can you imagine a Junior Monster Scouts book without Castle Dracula? Junior Monster Scouts without Castle Dracula? Can you imagine the villagers looking out their windows and instead of seeing the towers and peaks of the place where help has always come from, they saw winding roller coasters and spinning wheel rides?

Franky shook his head.

"No way," he said. "It's not too late to show that Gilbert Rutherford Weatherspan the Third that Castle Dracula is not just some building to be turned into whatever he wants. We'll show him that Castle Dracula is what holds this whole valley together. It's a symbol, a landmark . . . an icon! The Junior Monster Scouts belong to Castle Dracula as much as Castle Dracula belongs to us!"

Dracula, Wolf Man, and Frankenstein thought for a minute. Suddenly, their sad faces were gone, and they looked quite determined.

"We'll slow those bulldozers down," said Wolf Man. "You Junior Monster Scouts organize a town meeting."

Dracula, Wolf Man, and Frankenstein marched down the Crooked Trail toward the smoke-belching, rumbling, grinding bulldozers.

"Boris," said Vampyra, "you and the rats head to the village. Get everyone to meet at Stargazer's Point."

"Fern, you take the Little Junior Monster Scouts to the lake and invite everyone who lives there to the meeting," said Wolfy.

"And we'll go visit Baron Von Grump," said Franky.

"Hands in," said Vampyra.

And together, the Junior Monster Scouts and Little Junior Monster Scouts all recited one of the scout mottos: "By paw or claw, by tooth or wing, Junior—*and Little Junior*—Monster Scouts can do anything!"

And off they went: Boris and the rats to the village; Fern and the rest of the Little Junior Monster Scouts to the lake; and Franky, Wolfy, and Vampyra to Baron Von Grump's windmill.

CHAPTER
5

WHILE DRACULA, WOLF MAN, AND Frankenstein kept the bulldozers from knocking down the Gloomy Woods—and paving a path for the other construction vehicles to move in and transform Castle Dracula—the Junior Monster Scouts (and Little Junior Monster Scouts—can't forget about them!) put their plan into action.

Boris and the rats went from house to house, spreading the word: Meet at

Stargazer's Point for an important meeting about Fun Park. Fern and the other cubs went to the lake houses and invited the people who lived there to the meeting.

And Franky, Wolfy, and Vampyra knocked on Baron Von Grump's door.

"Go away!" said Baron Von Grump from inside his windmill.

"Caw!" said Edgar. That meant "Leave us alone!"

Franky knocked again.

"I don't want to hear any more about your roads, or bridges, or bypasses!" said Baron Von Grump. "And I certainly don't want to hear any more noise!"

"Caw! Caw!" ("And we do *not* want to hear about your tunnels, either," said Edgar.)

"Baron Von Grump," said Vampyra, "it's us."

"Us who?"

"The Junior Monster Scouts," said Wolfy.

Baron Von Grump threw open his shutters and looked out.

"So it is," he said. "What do you want? Can't you see they're building and banging and bulldozing everywhere you look?"

"That's why we're here," said Franky. "We're going to have a meeting at Stargazer's Point to come up with a plan."

"A plan for what?" asked Baron Von Grump. He was suddenly very interested. He was so interested that he gave his beard a few tugs.

"A plan to stop Fun Park from taking over and ruining our home," said Vampyra.

"And your peace and quiet," said Wolfy.

Baron Von Grump smiled ever so slightly.

"That," he said, "is music to my ears."

And if you know Baron Von Grump, you know how serious he is about his music.

. . .

Let's pause for a minute and take a look at the very busy, very hectic scene unfolding here. You might be surprised that this was happening so fast. It certainly seems like we snapped our fingers and *poof!* Construction was happening. It's enough to make you dizzy. I know my head is spinning. But it wasn't a matter of snapping fingers; it was all part of Gilbert's plan. He was a mover and shaker, and whenever he made his mind up about something, he wanted it done and he wanted it done yesterday. So that was the situation: There were builders building, cranes lifting, pavers paving roads, construction workers in hard hats and tool belts hammering and drilling and measuring. There were new roads that went this way and that way and every which way. There was a bridge being built *over* the village. There were giant billboards being put in place that advertised FUN PARK: SO. MUCH. FUN! And this one: RIDE THE DUELING DRAGONS COASTER! HUNDREDS OF FEET IN THE AIR! And this billboard: DARE TO ENTER THE TOWER TWISTER! There was noise, noise, noise, noise . . . and everywhere you looked, the village was no longer looking like the village we all know and love. Things were changing. The nooks and crannies that the villagers knew, that they were familiar with, that they loved, were suddenly not the same. If you don't know what a nook or a cranny is, well, I suppose you could ask your parent or teacher or librarian. They'd be happy to tell you what a nook and a cranny is. I'd tell you, but we need to be on time for that meeting that is going to take place very soon.

And speaking of the villagers, they were following the mayor, who, in turn, was following Boris and the rats. They set off for Stargazer's Point, trying to avoid dump trucks and forklifts.

Fern and the other Little Junior Monster Scouts led the people from the lake to Stargazer's Point. They had to walk around a gaggle of engineers trying to decide whether they should build one bridge across the lake or two, or maybe bridges over bridges. . . . They *really* liked their bridges. After all, they reasoned, they needed lots of ways for people to get to the new castle-themed Fun Park!

And finally, there were the Junior Monster Scouts with Baron Von Grump and Edgar.

"Snurgle Glop!" said the Trash Heap (if you're not familiar with the Trash Heap, see book #5, *Trash Heap of Terror*—but don't worry, she's nice), welcoming everyone to Stargazer's Point.

Franky, Wolfy, and Vampyra stepped forward.

"Friends and neighbors—" Franky began.

BEEP-BEEP-BEEP-BEEP.

A dump truck was backing up and making a very loud noise.

"We asked you all here tod—"

RUMBLE-RUMBLE-GRUMBLE-RUMBLE.

Several concrete mixer trucks drove by.

"—today to stop Fun Park—"

"But why would we want to stop them?" asked a villager in a straw hat. "They're going to have two roller coasters that look like dragons, spinning around each other!"

"The least they could do is make a giant Frankenstein roller coaster or something," mumbled Franky.

"And a ride that spins you around so fast, it'll make you sick!" said a villager with two pigs on leashes.

"Well, that doesn't sound fun at all," said Wolfy.

"And jugglers on stilts!" said a fisherman with his fishing pole over his shoulder.

Vampyra groaned.

"But we don't need all those things," she said. "We were just fine before, and if they make Castle Dracula into an amusement park, they'll be taking away the headquarters of the Junior Monster Scouts. Think of all the times we've helped you solve your problems."

The villagers and lakeside people all nodded and murmured and scratched their heads. They heard what the Junior Monster Scouts were saying, but they were also a bit under Gilbert's spell—he made those rides seem very thrilling and super exciting.

The Junior Monster Scouts did not know what to do. Between the excitement of the villagers and the noise of the trucks and construction, no one was actually *hearing* what they were trying to say.

Imagine trying to tell someone something and every time you tried to speak, a dog started barking, or someone started banging a drum, or maybe turned on the vacuum. And then, when you *could* be heard, the other person wasn't really listening. That is frustrating!

However, the mayor decided that this was a good time to be a leader. He stepped up, cleared his throat, and said . . .

CHAPTER 6

"VILLAGERS, PEOPLE OF THE LAKE, monsters, and Baron Von Grump, I—"

The villagers and the people who lived by the lake clapped one another on the back and grinned. They went on and on about all the fun they were going to have and which ride they were going to go on first and how tall the juggler on stilts would be and if there would be lemonade-flavored cotton candy or not.

The mayor, Baron Von Grump, Edgar, the Junior (and Little Junior) Monster Scouts, the rats, and the Trash Heap gathered.

"Well, that didn't work," said Boris the rat.

"Whatever are we going to do?" asked the mayor, wringing his hat in his hand.

"We need a better plan, a scheme!" said Baron Von Grump. "I want this nonsense to stop so that I can be alone, in my windmill, with my violin."

"Caw?" said Edgar. That meant "What about me?"

"And Edgar, of course," said Baron Von Grump.

But just as they were discussing this, the WHUMP-WHUMP-WHUMP of the helicopter sounded overhead. It landed right by them, on Stargazer's Point. The steps unfolded and Gilbert Rutherford Weatherspan the Third, with his fancy suit, perfect hair, and extremely white teeth, stepped out. Arthur, clipboard in hand, was right behind him.

"Good afternoon," said Gilbert. He adjusted his tie. "I see you've gathered to celebrate with us!"

"Celebrate what?" said Baron Von Grump, scowling.

"Oh . . . you didn't know?" said Gilbert. "Tell them, Arthur."

Arthur stepped around Gilbert and glanced at his clipboard.

"You are standing on the site of the future Fun Park airport," he said. "Before you know it, planes from all over the world will be zooming in and zooming out, bringing people from out *there* to have fun *here*, at the new castle-themed amusement park."

He reached into the helicopter and produced a pole with a little flag on it. It read PROPERTY OF FUN PARK.

Gilbert grinned. "Isn't that fantastic?" he asked.

"No!" said Vampyra. "It isn't!"

Gilbert and Arthur looked confused. "It isn't?" they said at the same time.

"It isn't!" Wolfy said. "This is the best place for watching shooting stars, making wishes, and howling at the moon!"

"This is where I like to bring my telescope to count the rings of Saturn," said Franky.

The mayor stepped forward. "It's such

a quiet, peaceful place. And there's such a wonderful view of that wonderful Castle Dracula."

"And speaking of Castle Dracula," said Vampyra, "we live in the castle. Where are we supposed to go? Where will we live? But most of all . . . our castle has been here for a long, long time. Even before the village was here. That's where we have our scout meetings. That's where we come up with plans to help those in need. Castle Dracula is where many fantastic inventions, discoveries, and solutions have come from!"

Gilbert Rutherford Weatherspan the Third crossed his arms and nodded. "I see," he said. "Arthur, take note of these citizens' concerns."

Arthur scribbled something down on his clipboard.

"Of course, they'll be ignored," said Gilbert. "But here, have a coupon for one free ride on the amazing Dueling Dragons roller coaster!"

He thrust a bunch of passes toward them and smiled. The sun glinted off his very white, very sparkly teeth.

"Villagers," he said, "people of the lake,

monsters, and Baron Von Grump, I—"

But the villagers and the people who lived by the lake were starting to leave.

"Okay then," he said, climbing back up the steps and into the helicopter. "Wonderful chat, very exciting, have a great day!"

WHUMP-WHUMP-WHUMP went the blades as the helicopter lifted into the sky and flew away.

Baron Von Grump, Edgar, the mayor, the Trash Heap and her family, Boris and the rats, and all the Monster Scouts stood there, staring at the flag stuck in the ground of Stargazer's Point.

Finally Fern, the leader of the Little Junior Monster Scouts, stepped up.

"I think I have an idea," she said.

CHAPTER

7

IT TURNS OUT THAT FERN HAD AN *excellent* idea. Actually, several ideas! And with everyone's help, the scouts would be able to take those ideas and, hopefully, stop Gilbert from taking over Castle Dracula and changing *everything*.

Want to know what her ideas were?

Me too! I guess we'll have to wait and see.

But we won't have to wait too long, because the Junior and Little Junior Monster Scouts were already putting the first part of their new plan into motion. Sure, they had not succeeded yet, but these are the Junior Monster Scouts we're talking about. They were not about to give up!

Baron Von Grump was quite impressed with Fern's idea.

"I think I have something to contribute," said Baron Von Grump. "Come along, Edgar."

"Caw!" said Edgar.

They both left for the windmill.

Franky, Wolfy, and Vampyra rushed back to Castle Dracula. They found an old tablecloth, some red paint, and some brushes. On the tablecloth, they painted, in BIG, red letters, FUN-CASTLE. And then under that, in EVEN BIGGER letters, they painted FREE FUN!

Franky asked the gargoyles if they'd fly halfway up the castle and then perch there and hold the banner. Of course they were happy to. They wanted to be a part of saving Castle Dracula and the rest of the land.

While the gargoyles got themselves settled, proudly displaying their FUN-CASTLE banner with the FREE FUN! announcement, the Junior Monster Scouts gathered a large inflatable ball, some old bowling pins, some Frisbees, a couple of Hula-Hoops, and a bunch of bean bags. All fun things!

That was the plan. They were going to have fun and games for all ages! Just like they'd done at so many other village celebrations. They'd have a riddle booth, just like when Neveen, their mummy exchange student friend and her sphinx, Cleo, came to visit. There would be a Snurgle Ball match, and unicycle races, and, of course, pudding tag. There'd also be Frisbee tag (for those who couldn't stop themselves from eating the pudding right away), and a Hula-Hoop contest, and bean bag tosses, and bowling with the giant inflatable ball.

They had just finished setting up their

games when Fern and the rest of the cubs, along with Boris and the rats, began to arrive. But they did not come empty-handed, oh no! They had cheese wheels and cheese wedges and even cheese balls. They had an old popcorn machine and buckets of kernels for popping. They had wagons for wagon rides and an old fun-house mirror.

"Where'd you get all this stuff?" Wolfy asked.

Boris shrugged. "Let's just say that they've got more cheese in that Cheese Storage Pyramid than they even know what to do with."

"And the popcorn machine?" asked Franky.

"That's from the Trash Heap," said Fern. "Still works!"

"But what about this fun-house mirror?"

asked Vampyra. She made a funny face in it.

One of the cubs grinned. "Baron Von Grump sent that. He said he was tired of looking at himself in it!" (See Junior Monster Scouts #4, *Monster of Disguise*, to read more about *that* story.)

"Well," said Wolfy, "let's get set up. There's FUN to be had!"

The rats and the Monster Scouts put out a table for cheese treats. They set up the popcorn machine. And finally, they stood the fun-house mirror up right in the middle of everything. The front lawn of Castle Dracula was filled with the promise of fun and games.

"Okay," said Vampyra. "Now we need to get everyone here."

Boris the rat grinned. "Leave that up to us," he said. "Come on, fellas!"

Boris and his rats scampered off toward the village and the lake.

The Junior and Little Junior Monster Scouts did not have to wait long. As soon as people heard from Boris and the rats that there was FREE FUN at Castle Dracula, they stopped what they were doing and hurried toward the castle. All this talk about FUN PARK and FUN had them eager with anticipation. They couldn't wait to have fun!

"Here they come," said Franky.

"Wow," said a man with a beard down to his knees. "Look at all these fun games!" He picked up a Frisbee and threw it to another villager. "Whee!"

"We can play . . . for *free?*" asked a woman with sunglasses too big for her face.

"One hundred percent free," said Vampyra.

"What about the cheese?" she asked.

"Free," said Vampyra. "Made right here, in the village!"

"The popcorn?"

"That's free too," said Vampyra, smiling.

"Let's start having fun now!" said a

woman with a pig pulling a cart. She stood in front of the mirror and stuck her tongue out while standing on one leg.

"We're even giving tours of the castle," said Wolfy. "We'll show you the tower and the library and the lab and even say hi to the gargoyles!"

The villagers were delighted. In all the time that they'd lived right next to one another, they'd never thought of asking to see the inside of Castle Dracula. And now they were going to get a tour by the Junior Monster Scouts themselves!

They bowled with the giant inflatable ball and challenged one another to Hula-Hoop contests to see who could Hula-Hoop the longest. They played Frisbee tag while laughing and cheering. They tossed bean bags for little prizes. They ate cheese balls and popcorn and played a round of "Guess That Cheese," a game where you are blindfolded and have to name the kind of cheese you are eating. They laughed at one another's images in the fun-house mirror.

In other words, they were having a *very* good time.

You may be wondering, at this point, What did Gilbert think? What did Gilbert Rutherford Weatherspan the Third think about all these villagers munching cheese, and touring the castle, and playing games?

"And they gave everyone *free* fun?" Gilbert asked.

Arthur shifted nervously and checked his clipboard.

"Yes, sir," he said.

"What *kind* of fun?" asked Gilbert.

Arthur checked his papers. "Many games and amusements."

Gilbert was not smiling.

Arthur cleared his throat. "And there were . . . um . . . tours of the castle."

"Tours of the castle!?" said Gilbert.

Arthur shuffled his feet.

"And a fun-house mirror," he said.

Gilbert was red with anger. One of the hairs on his perfectly groomed head fell out of place.

"Ready the helicopter," he said. "No one out-funs Fun Park!"

CHAPTER 8

THE HELICOPTER WHUMP-WHUMP-WHUMPED its way toward the village. You know who was inside it. Perfect hair, teeth entirely too white, fancy suit . . . that's right! Gilbert Rutherford Weatherspan the Third . . . and, of course, Arthur. And his clipboard.

But the Junior and Little Junior Monster Scouts were way ahead of Gilbert. They knew that once they started providing free fun for the villagers, Gilbert Rutherford

Weatherspan the Third was sure to make a visit. And to visit, he'd have to use his helicopter.

That's where Baron Von Grump and Edgar came in, along with their windmill. Baron Von Grump had always been a bit of a planner and a schemer. Most of the time, he was planning and scheming to chase the villagers away, or foil the plans of the Junior Monster Scouts, but this time he was making his plans and schemes to help them. And himself, of course. After all, there was banging and drilling and hammering and sawing, beeping and bumping and clanging and thumping, right outside his normally quiet living room. If you know anything about Baron Von Grump, you know that he does not like noise. Not one bit.

So, you might ask, what was Baron Von Grump and Edgar's part in this plan? Let's take a look, shall we? But wait a minute— let me just go and get a glass of cold, refreshing caramel lemonade.

WHUMP-WHUMP-WHUMP.

The helicopter drew nearer.

Just one sec and I'll be back with my— what? You can't wait? The helicopter is on its way? Fine, fine. I guess I'll have to wait for my cold, refreshing caramel lemonade.

Baron Von Grump and Edgar were given the very important job of making sure that Gilbert and Arthur could not land their helicopter and try to convince the villagers that their village was old, and boring, and quiet, and quaint.

In order to pull that off, they needed some strong wind. Wind so strong that it would be impossible for the helicopter to land. How do you think they could manage that? What could they possibly use to create WIND?

Remember where Baron Von Grump and Edgar live.

That's right! The windmill. You are very clever, my friend.

Edgar took the power cable from Baron Von Grump and flew up to the top of the windmill. There, he plugged it into the hub, where the four windmill fan blades were fastened. The hub was what turned when winds came along, pushing the fan blades.

But that alone would not be a strong enough wind to stop a helicopter from landing. That's where the power cable came in.

Baron Von Grump took the other end out to where the construction was happening.

"Hello there," he said to a very important-looking person in a tie and a bright yellow hard hat.

The important-looking person barely looked up from the blueprints he was studying.

"Hello back," said the very important person in the tie and bright yellow hard hat. He had a name tag that read WALTER.

"I was wondering if I could just plug this cord into your generator for a little bit, Walter," said Baron Von Grump. "I could use a little extra energy, and you seem to have quite a bit."

Walter lowered the blueprints just enough to look at Baron Von Grump.

"You want to plug your cord into our generator?" he asked.

"Yes," said Baron Von Grump. He smiled as big a smile as he could manage. That was a very hard thing for Baron Von Grump to do. He was not accustomed to smiling. At least not, especially not, at other people.

"I'm afraid you cannot," said Walter.

"Cannot?" asked Baron Von Grump. His smile slipped. The entire plan hinged on getting the power to the windmill.

WHUMP-WHUMP-WHUMP.

"Cannot," repeated Walter.

"Oh," said Baron Von Grump. "And why is that?"

"Because you're not wearing a hard hat."

"I see," said Baron Von Grump.

Edgar, who had been circling overhead, heard this as well. He knew just what to do. He swooped by a nearby equipment locker and snatched up a spare hard hat.

A few moments later, a yellow hard hat fell from the sky and landed on Baron Von Grump's head.

"Not wearing a hard hat?" Baron Von Grump asked. "Then what do you call this?"

He pointed to his head.

"That is a very fine-looking hard hat," said Walter. "Plug your cord in, sir!"

Baron Von Grump grinned and plugged

the cord into the generator. The windmill blades began to turn faster, and faster, and faster, until they were turning so fast that a superstrong wind blew across the entire land, right over the village, right toward Castle Dracula, but most importantly, right under the hovering helicopter.

The helicopter wobbled in the air. No

matter how hard they tried to land, they could not. Every time they got just a little close, the breeze pushed them right back up into the air.

"Get us as close as you can!" Gilbert hollered to the pilot. It was hard to hear over the wind, and the windmill, and the helicopter blades WHUMP-WHUMP-WHUMPing.

Gilbert nudged Arthur.

"Hand me the megaphone," he said.

Arthur handed Gilbert the megaphone.

"Attention, villagers!" Gilbert said, pointing the megaphone down at the village and the villagers, who were just now gathering to see what was going on with the wobbling, warbling helicopter over their homes.

"What's he saying?" asked one villager.

"Can't hear him over all that whooshing and whumping," said another.

"Ya gotta land so we can hear what you're saying!" hollered a third villager.

Gilbert tried again.

"Our fun is the best fun!" he said into the megaphone.

"Sour buns?" said a villager, scratching his head.

"Our fun!" said Gilbert.

"Flour puns?" asked another villager.

"OUR FUN!" Gilbert hollered into the megaphone as loud as he could.

"Ohhhhhhhh," said another villager. "No thank you. I had so much fun that I'm funned out for the day. And boy, was that castle tour something special! I even pressed some buttons in Dr. Frankenstein's lab!"

Gilbert was not happy, not happy at all. But no matter how unhappy he was, the helicopter had to leave. There was just too much wind to stay in the air, and too much wind to land.

The helicopter veered off and WHUMP-WHUMP-WHUMPed away.

CHAPTER 9

THAT MIGHT HAVE TAKEN CARE OF GILBERT and Fun Park (for now), but there was still the problem of all the ongoing construction. There were roads and bridges getting ready to be built, tunnels marked out for digging, and even flags in place where the runway for the new airport was going to go. The workers were working, the cranes were lifting, and the trucks were rumbling. If nothing was done soon, it would be too late. There would not be one speck of grass left on Stargazer's Point, not a tree left standing in the Gloomy Woods, not a river still running, a waterfall falling, or a lake left clean and sparkling! And if those bulldozers got back to bulldozing, there might not be much left of Castle Dracula. Not one tower, not the laboratory, not the grand hall or a single gargoyle.

But Fern had a plan for this as well. She was very clever, like you. She'd learned a lot by watching and listening to the Junior Monster Scouts. This part of the plan fell to the mayor. But first she wanted to check with her big brother and the other Junior Monster Scouts. They always knew what to do!

Fern found Vampyra, Wolfy, and Franky

showing another group of villagers around the castle.

"And this is where we hold our Junior Monster Scout meetings," said Franky to the group.

Fern waited until they were done and then told the Junior Monster Scouts what she was thinking. They thought it was a pretty clever idea, so Fern hurried off to share her idea with the mayor.

He was also quite impressed and sprang to action.

He put on his best hat and coat. He combed his mustache and brushed his beard. He even put on a fancy bow tie, a purple one with bright green polka dots and a hummingbird in the middle. Once he was dressed in his finest, most important-looking clothes (his hat was especially magnificent, being half as tall as he was and wrapped with a green band that held not one but three large peacock feathers), he gathered up his papers and stepped out into the village.

The villagers were very impressed with how nice the mayor looked, and they did not hesitate to tell him as much.

"My, oh my," said a villager, still munching on a cup of cheese balls, "don't you just look like a million bucks!"

"Why, thank you," said the mayor.

"You must be on official business, Mister Mayor," said another villager, finishing their popcorn.

"I am!" said the mayor. "Very official. The most official!"

"That is the best hat I've ever seen!" said a third villager, Hula-Hooping with the Hula-Hoop he'd won from the contest. "And I've seen *a lot* of hats."

The mayor tipped his hat to the villager and smiled. He was feeling very confident now. He was feeling so confident that he walked right up to the very important person in the tie and yellow hard hat holding the blueprints (the very same person Baron Von Grump had spoken to—Walter).

"Can I help you?" asked Walter. He lowered his blueprints and gave the mayor his full attention. After all, the mayor looked very fancy, and very official. It would be almost impossible to *not* give him your full attention. Especially with that hat!

"Yes," said the mayor, standing as tall as he could and squaring his shoulders. "Yes, you can."

"And what might you need?" Walter asked.

"You can stop all this racket and ruckus immediately," said the mayor.

"Racket and ruckus?" asked Walter. "You mean . . . *construction?*"

"That is exactly what I mean," said the mayor. "Don't even consider digging up one more speck of dirt, or disturbing one more blade of grass."

"Stop constructing the roads and the buildings? The bridges and the runway?"

"All of it," said the mayor. He adjusted his bow tie. "Immediately. At once. This very second."

Walter looked very confused. It was not every day that a man in a very tall hat with not one but three peacock feathers suddenly told you to stop building the things you were supposed to build.

"But . . . but we can't," said Walter. "We have a contract. We have to build these roads and bridges, buildings and runways, tunnels and traffic circles, for Fun Park."

"That may be true," said the mayor, "but it is my understanding that you cannot work on holidays. Isn't that true? Aren't you required to give your workers time off on holidays?"

"Well . . . yes," said Walter. "But today isn't a holiday."

"It isn't?" asked the mayor with a twinkle in his eye. Oh, he was feeling *very* confident now.

You see, he had a little secret, and that secret was part of the latest "Save Castle Dracula" plan.

"Not that I know of," said Walter.

The mayor produced his very official papers with a very official stamp on the front page.

"As mayor of the village, and elected representative of the lake and Castle Dracula, I have declared today, and *every* day after, to be Good Neighbor Day. An official holiday that celebrates our neighbors and spreads goodwill and kindness to all."

He held the papers out for Walter to read.

"Well, that is very official," Walter said.

"Even has a stamp on it."

"That it does," said the mayor, feeling quite proud of himself. "And in the spirit of Good Neighbor Day, might I extend a hearty handshake to you, Walter, for the hard work your crew has been preparing to do."

Walter shook the mayor's hand.

"That is very kind of you, and in the spirit of the holiday, I will tell *you*, Mister Mayor, that that is the finest hat I have ever seen. And I have seen a lot of hats."

Walter turned around to the workers and whistled very loudly. The hammerers stopped hammering, and the machines stopped rumbling and beeping. Workers stopped drilling and sawing, carrying and constructing. They all stopped and listened to Walter.

"All right, everyone," Walter said. "No more building! It was just brought to my attention that today is a village, lake, and castle holiday. And you know what that means . . . can't work on a holiday!"

"But what about tomorrow?" asked one of the workers.

"Still a holiday," said Walter.

"And the next day?" asked another worker.

"Holiday," said Walter.

"Two weeks from now?" asked a third, putting his hammer down.

"Holiday," said Walter. "Good Neighbor Day. Every day. Looks like our work here is done. Pack up your tools and turn your trucks around!"

The workers quickly set to packing everything up. Every screw, every nail, every hammer and saw.

They closed up their toolboxes and turned off their generators. They turned their trucks around. They even took off their hard hats.

With a wave and a few honks from the big trucks, the crew rode away, leaving the village and the valley.

CHAPTER
10

AHHHH . . . TAKE A SECOND AND LISTEN. Hear that? Quiet. No helicopters, no work trucks, no construction.

However, things weren't quite settled yet. The first thing the workers had built was the huge Fun Park welcome center and gift shop. It didn't have any stuff in it yet, but it was there, right outside the village: a building designed to look like a much smaller version of the castle. A statue of the Fun

Park mascot (a zebra wearing goggles and purple shorts) stood proudly out front.

The workers may have been gone, but Fun Park was not. And neither was Gilbert Rutherford Weatherspan the Third. He might not have been able to land his helicopter in the village, but that did not stop him from arriving in his jeep.

Franky, Wolfy, and Vampyra had just reached the village when Gilbert came around the corner with Arthur.

The mayor was also there to greet Gilbert Rutherford Weatherspan the Third. The villagers had assembled as well.

"Good Neighbor Day to you, Junior Monster Scouts," said the mayor.

"And to you, Mister Mayor," said Vampyra.

The jeep screeched to a halt in front of the welcome center and gift shop. Arthur leaped out, hurried around to the other side, and opened Gilbert's door for him.

"Where are my workers!?" Gilbert said, stepping out of the jeep. "Why aren't they building? These roads and bridges aren't finished! No tunnels have been dug! There's no runway for airplanes!"

"The workers went home," said Franky.

Gilbert looked confused. He turned to Arthur.

"Did we tell the workers to go home?" asked Gilbert.

Arthur checked his clipboard.

"No," he said. "We most certainly did not."

Gilbert gritted his extremely white teeth.

"Then why," he said through his gritted teeth, "are they not here, working?"

"Because it's a holiday," said Vampyra.

"Good Neighbor Day!" said Wolfy.

"That's ridiculous," said Gilbert. "I've never heard of that holiday, and I know holidays. I have to know holidays so that I can offer holiday sales and discounts. Plus, there are holiday parades and holiday shows."

The mayor held out his official papers.

"It's a new holiday," said the mayor. "Started today."

Gilbert snatched the papers from the mayor and thrust them at Arthur.

"Read this," he said.

Arthur read the papers and handed them back to the mayor.

"I'm afraid it's official and legal, sir," Arthur said. "Celebrated today and . . . every day after. A constant village, lake, and castle holiday."

Gilbert slowly nodded. "I see what you're doing here, and I must admit, it's very clever. But I'm afraid that won't stop us. Our welcome center and gift shop is built, as you can see, and even though the roads aren't finished, we'll just bring people to the castle by jeep! We're still going to build our park in *your* castle. Fun Park cannot be stopped! Soon your precious castle will be packed with roller coasters and long lines! Out with the old and in with the new!"

He leaned his head back and laughed a long, sinister laugh.

He stopped for a moment and nudged Arthur.

"Why aren't you laughing? When I laugh, you laugh. We talked about this, Arthur!"

"Oh yes, right, of course, sir," said Arthur.

Then Gilbert leaned his head back and laughed again and Arthur laughed along with him.

"All we need to open the store is to pass our health and safety inspection," said Gilbert. "Here comes the inspector now!"

A truck pulled up to the group and stopped. It had a logo on the side that read HEALTH AND SAFETY INSPECTOR. A woman with tinted sunglasses and a clipboard of her own stepped out.

"Let's make this quick," she said. "I'm a very busy woman."

"Of course," said Gilbert. "Right this way."

He and Arthur led the inspector toward the front door of the welcome center and gift shop.

The Junior Monster Scouts and the mayor stood nervously. What could they do? How could they stop the inspector from approving this site and letting Gilbert destroy their beloved castle?

Vampyra stepped before the assembled villagers. "Friends," she said, "if we let Fun Park take over Castle Dracula, we'll have no place to call home. We've always lived there, right next door, your good neighbors, eager to help you when you needed help."

Wolfy stepped up next to her.

"Whenever you had a problem, we helped you fix it," he said. "We've always been there to lend a paw. Like when the rats were scaring you out of your village, or when the power went out during the village's birthday celebration, or when the storm blocked up the river."

"We've shared laughs and scares, plenty of excitement, and lots of stories together," said Franky. "Like when we solved the trash heap monster problem, or when everyone didn't answer the sphinx's riddles and was turned to stone, or when we brought all the Grumps together for their big reunion party. You can't let them take our castle. You can't let them take away our Crooked Trail and Gloomy Woods. Stargazer's Point and the Cheese Storage Pyramid. The farms and fields of the village and Baron

Von Grump's humble windmill. And you can't let them take the heartbeat of it all, our castle, Castle Dracula."

The mayor stepped up too, fancy hat in hand. He wiped a tear from his eye. "They're right, you know. The Junior Monster Scouts have helped us time and time again. Now it's time we help them. What do you say?"

The villagers were quiet for a second. They looked at the zebra statue with the goggles and the purple pants, and then they looked at the Junior (and Little Junior) Monster Scouts. Finally, one villager with a chicken tucked under his arm nodded and said, "You've always been kind to us. I won't stand for Castle Dracula being turned into some amusement park."

"And I can't think of you having to leave your home," said a villager with fancy suspenders, "and not being our good neighbors anymore."

Another villager tugged his beard and said, "You've saved the day so many times, the least we can do is help to save yours! Why, heck, what's yours is ours and what's ours is yours. We're a community. We're a family!"

One by one, villagers stepped forward to thank the Monster Scouts and to tell them how much they appreciated them, and their families, and Castle Dracula. And one by one, they marched forward and stood between Gilbert Rutherford Weatherspan the Third, Arthur, and the inspector, and the door to the welcome center.

"Get out of our way!" screamed Gilbert Rutherford Weatherspan the Third. "This is official business!"

The villagers did not get out of their way.

"You can't possibly have fun without us!" he shouted.

"That's not true," said the chicken-holding villager. "We had plenty of fun today, and we didn't need Fun Park to have it."

"And we didn't have to chase our friends out of their homes either," said another.

Arthur and the inspector stood there, arms crossed, unable to enter the welcome center.

"I suppose this means we failed our inspection?" Arthur asked.

"Correct," said the inspector. "I'm a very busy woman." She stamped FAILED on the inspection papers and handed them to Arthur. She climbed into her truck and drove off.

Gilbert threw up his hands in frustration and stormed off toward his jeep.

Arthur stood there a moment, watching his boss.

"I guess you won't be opening after all," said the mayor.

"I guess not," said Arthur. A little smile spread across his face. "And you know what . . . that's okay. It's nice to see him not win for once."

"Arthur!" Gilbert yelled from the jeep. "Get in this vehicle this second and drive us out of here!"

Arthur sighed and looked at his clipboard.

"It seems," said the mayor, "that we may be in need of someone with dedication and strong organizational skills to lead the way in taking down these half-built bridges and removing these unfinished roads."

"Are you offering me a *job*?" Arthur asked.

The Junior Monster Scouts had not seen this coming! To tell you the truth, neither did I.

"Arthur, how would you like to be chief engineer of Fun Park removal?" the mayor asked.

BEEEEEEEEEEEEEEEPPPPPPPPPPPPPPPPPP.

Gilbert blared on the horn.

"We're leaving, Arthur!" Gilbert hollered.

"Excuse me one moment," Arthur said. He marched over to the jeep.

"It's about time," Gilbert said.

Arthur handed Gilbert his clipboard.

"I quit," he said. Then he returned to the mayor and said, "I accept."

Arthur and the mayor shook hands, and

the Junior Monster Scouts clapped and cheered.

You know who wasn't cheering, don't you? Gilbert Rutherford Weatherspan the Third. He shook his fist out the window.

"You haven't heard the last from—oh, confound it, how do you drive this thing? Why is it so bumpy? Why are there so many buttons?"

Gilbert Rutherford Weatherspan the Third drove off in a zigzag pattern, bouncing and bumping along.

"Goodbye and good riddance, Gilbert Rutherford Weatherspan the Third," Baron Von Grump called after him.

"Caw!" said Edgar. That meant "And please don't visit ever again!"

Gilbert, of course, was wrong. That *was* the last they heard from him, and from Fun Park, but let's not get ahead of ourselves.

CHAPTER 11

LIKE ALL ADVENTURES WITH THE Junior Monster Scouts, this one would not be complete without a Junior Monster Scout meeting. But this time, instead of holding it at Castle Dracula, they held it right in the middle of the village!

Everyone was there for the big celebration. After all, they had all worked together to save their community! The villagers were there, as well as the mayor, the Junior and Little Junior Monster Scouts, Dracula, Frankenstein, and Wolf Man. Dr. Frankenstein and Igor Senior and Igor Junior. Aunts Hemlock, Belladonna, and Moonflower. Boris and the rats. The Trash Heap and her children. Arthur. And yes, even Baron Von Grump and Edgar. It was quite a gathering!

"Everyone, everyone, can I have your attention?" said Dracula.

The crowd quieted.

"I'd like to begin by wishing you all a Good Neighbor Day!"

Everyone cheered and smiled and high-fived.

"Tonight, we won't be giving our scouts any merit badges," said Wolf Man.

There was a loud gasp from the crowd. The Junior Monster Scouts looked surprised. They'd worked so hard, and they still had a little bit of room on their sashes. The Little Junior Monster Scouts looked from Wolfy, Vampyra, and Franky to Wolf Man, Dracula, and Frankenstein.

"Instead," said Frankenstein, "we'll be giving them something much bigger. Vampyra, Wolfy, Franky, please step forward."

The Junior Monster Scouts stepped into the middle of the gathering.

Frankenstein continued, "For what you did here, and for all the times you have helped when needed, solved problems when they arose, and generally done genuine good deeds, you are hereby granted full senior scout status! From now on, you will lead all scouts, give all merit badges, and be an example for those scouts who follow."

Wolf Man stepped forward and placed the sash of the Senior Monster Scout on each of them.

"And you, Little Junior Monster Scouts," said Dracula. "You are hereby promoted to the rank of *Junior* Monster Scout! Under the leadership of Vampyra, Wolfy, and Franky, you will work on achieving your merit badges and following the Monster Scout oath."

Fern and the rest of the cubs all jumped and clapped.

Wolfy presented each of the cubs with their new Junior Monster Scout sash.

The mayor stepped forward. "And Fern," he said, "for your brilliant plan to save us from Fun Park, I declare you Village Champion. Arthur has designed a new fountain for the center of our humble village, and a plaque, in your honor, will be placed upon it.

"Boris, rats, Trash Heap," continued the

mayor, "know that you are all friends of the village and welcome here at any time. Trash Heap, our trash is your trash. Boris, rats, our cheese is your cheese."

The villagers cheered. Boris, the rats, and the Trash Heap all bowed in honor.

"But there's one more person to be recognized," said Franky, stepping forward.

"Someone who used to always grumble and complain, plot and scheme, scowl and stomp," said Wolfy.

"But in the end, he showed us all that we can be good neighbors," said Vampyra. "Baron Von Grump, we'd like to thank you and Edgar for showing us that despite our differences, there is still one thing that unites us . . . and that is caring for the neighborhood we share. For our little valley. Thank you, Baron Von Grump and Edgar, and happy Good Neighbor Day to you."

"Oh, it's . . . it's nothing," said Baron Von Grump, waving off the compliment.

"Caw!" said Edgar. That meant "Think nothing of it."

But wait . . . was that a tear in the baron's eye?

Vampyra leaned over to Fern and whispered in her ear.

Fern stepped forward and said, "Okay, everyone, please join us in reciting the Junior Monster Scout oath, because you are *all* honorary Monster Scouts!"

You can imagine how excited everyone was to hear that! They crowded in and, with Fern in the lead, recited the Junior Monster Scout oath (with a few additions):

I promise to be nice, not scary. To help, not harm. To always try to do my best. I am a monster, a villager, a friend, and a neighbor, and I am friendly, not mean. We are all Junior Monster Scouts!

All of us, dear reader. Even you. *Especially* you.

JUNIOR MONSTER SCOUT
· HANDBOOK ·

The Junior Monster Scout oath:

I promise to be nice, not scary. To help, not harm. To always try my best to do my best.

I am a monster, but I am not mean. I am a Junior Monster Scout or Little Junior Monster Scout!

Junior Monster Scout mottos:

By paw or claw, by tooth or wing, Junior Monster Scouts can do anything!

Never say "never" when friends work together!

By tooth or wing, by paw or claw, a Junior Monster Scout does it all!

When someone else is in trouble, we help them out on the double!

Any problem can be solved when all your friends get involved!

No one is left out when you're with the Junior Monster Scouts!

Little Junior Monster Scouts are kind and lend a hand, especially to those who are strangers in our land.

Junior Monster Scouts tell the truth, with every fang and every tooth.

No job is too big, no task is too small, when the Junior Monster Scouts get the call.

Small or big, short or tall, a Junior Monster Scout is there to help all!

I promise to be nice, not scary. To help, not harm. To always try to do my best. I am a monster, a villager, a friend, and a neighbor, and I am friendly, not mean. We are all Junior Monster Scouts!

Junior Monster Scout laws:

Be Kind—A scout treats others the way they want to be treated.

Be Friendly—A scout is open to everyone, no matter how different they are.

Be Helpful—A scout goes out of their way to do good deeds for others . . . without expecting a reward.

Be Careful—A scout thinks about what they say or do *before* they do it.

Be a Good Listener—A scout listens to what others have to say.

Be Brave—A scout does what is right, even if they are afraid, and a scout makes the right decisions . . . even if no one else does.

Be Trustworthy—A scout does what they say they will do, even if it is difficult.

Be Loyal—A scout is a good friend and will always be there for you when you need them.

Special awards:

Village Champion

· ACKNOWLEDGMENTS ·

Book ten . . . wow. Ten Junior Monster Scouts books! I am so grateful for having been able to bring these little monsters to life, to put them on the page . . . put them in your hearts and imaginations and on your shelves. But just like we've witnessed here, in this book, wonderful things like this only happen with the support and help of your own village. So, let me thank my village:

Jessica—my world. My everything. I love you!

Jennifer—agent extraordinaire! Your support and excitement for my imagination and my stories is wonderful. Here's to many more books!

Linda—you started this ball rolling and you've always been in my corner. Thank you.

Karen—we're quite the team, aren't we? Thanks for championing me and helping me become a better writer.

Marlene and Tom, Caroline and Jeff, Kirsten and Jim—our local independent bookstores who celebrated my first book launch with me, let Jess and me get married in the shop, brought me goodies when I was sick, and have always promoted, celebrated, and supported us. Thank you!

Our children, Shane, Zach, Logan, Ainsley,

Sawyer, and Braeden—we love you all so much and honestly, wish you would read more, lol.

Becca, Josh, Maddie, and Lena—what would we do without you guys? Love, love, love. 10/3!

Mom and Dad—thanks for your love and for letting my imagination do what it needed to, even when it scared you, lol.

Kim and Diana—thank you for being there for us and, most importantly, for Jess when she needed an ear the most in the darkest of moments. Twice.

Aunt Marion—thanks for buying me monster toys and sharing the black-and-white classics!

Lisa, Amy, Tom, Sharon, and Kathi—my mentors . . . I learned so much from each of you!

Ethan—how'd I get so lucky as to have you as my illustrator? Thanks, man! You rock!

And finally, to you, the reader—thank you for being a part of this world and for taking the time to sit down with my books, share in the stories, and celebrate the adventures of the Junior Monster Scouts!

READ THE FIRST
JUNIOR MONSTER SCOUTS BOOK!

WOLFY TOOK A DEEP BREATH. HE LOOKED to the sky. He leaned way back and let out the biggest, longest, loudest howl he could. It was a very good howl. It was such a good howl that it went right past the forest, over the covered bridge, through the village, and all the way to the Old Windmill.

"That was a good one!" said Franky Stein.

"I'll bet they could hear that howl all the way back at the castle!" said Vampyra.

"Thanks!" said Wolfy. He was very proud of himself. Tonight was the Junior Monster Scouts meeting, and Wolfy wanted to earn his Howling Merit Badge.

In fact, Wolfy's howl was such a good howl that it reached right through the open window of the Old Windmill, right into the ears of Baron Von Grump.

Baron Von Grump was always grumpy. Everything about him was grumpy. Even his eyebrows were grumpy. They were like two big, black, bushy, *grumpy* caterpillars crawling across his forehead. They were even blacker than Edgar, his pet crow.

"What was that *noise*?" he sneered. "That sounded like a howl. A *monstrous* howl. Oh, how I despise those wretched monsters!"

Edgar hopped onto the windowsill and peered out over the village. "Caw, caw!" Edgar did not like monsters either.

Baron Von Grump did not like noise. Baron Von Grump did not like anything, really, except for playing his violin and making plans. Baron Von Grump *loved* making plans. He loved that almost as much as he loved playing his violin.

So you see, Baron Von Grump loved *two* things. And everything else, he did not. Okay, he loved Edgar, too. *Three* things. Baron Von Grump loved three things.

Baron Von Grump looked out his window and glared at the village. Edgar glared with him.

Today was the village cheese festival, and

all of the villagers were busy setting up.

"Look at them!" he said. "Smiling, talking, singing, why . . . they're even chewing gum! I cannot stand when people chew gum . . . or sing, or talk, or smile. These villagers are almost as bad as those miserable monsters."

See? Baron Von Grump did not like anything besides making plans and his violin and Edgar. With all of this noise Baron Von Grump could not concentrate. If he could not concentrate, he could not play his violin. If he could not play his violin, he would become even grumpier than the grump he already was. And *that* is a *lot* of grump.

"I have a plan!" he said with a sly smirk.

"Caw! Caw!" said Edgar.

A plan! This made Baron Von Grump happy for one half of a second.

Make a smile. Just a little one. Barely twitch the corners of your mouth. Now stop. That was how long Baron Von Grump was happy. That was not very long, was it?

Edgar hopped onto Baron Von Grump's shoulder.

Baron Von Grump slammed his shutters closed. He knew just what to do to get rid of all of those smiling, talking, singing, gum-chewing villagers. He knew just how to chase them away.

MEET ASTRID!

SHE'S A GIRL WITH BIG DREAMS OF BEING THE FIRST ASTRONAUT WITH HEARING AIDS IN SPACE!

EBOOK EDITIONS AVAILABLE
ALADDIN
SIMONANDSCHUSTER.COM/KIDS

MEET JUNIOR MONSTER SCOUTS WOLFY, FRANKY, AND VAMPYRA! CAN THEY BEAT THE CRANKY BARON VON GRUMP AND EARN THEIR MERIT BADGES?

The Monster Squad

Crash! Bang! Boo!

It's Raining Bats and Frogs!

Monster of Disguise

Trash Heap of Terror

Curse of the Crummy Mummy!

Chiller Thriller!

The Rottenest Reunion

The Incredible Shrinking Grump

Castle of Schemes and Dreams

EBOOK EDITIONS AVAILABLE

Aladdin
simonandschuster.com/kids

Welcome to Wolver Hollow, where strange, creepy, and weird things happen!

EBOOK EDITIONS AVAILABLE
Aladdin · simonandschuster.com/kids

Meet the latest superheroes:
THE HUNGER HEROES!

Mr. Toots the bean, Chip Ninja, Tammy the tomato, and Leonard the wedge of cheddar cheese come to the rescue of hungry kids everywhere!

EBOOK EDITIONS AVAILABLE
Aladdin
simonandschuster.com/kids

Follow twins Emma and Martín on their magical adventures into a book of Mexican legends!

EBOOK EDITIONS AVAILABLE
Aladdin | simonandschuster.com/kids